Br'er Rabbit Captured!

JEAN CASSELS

Walker & Company   New York

"Pack your bag, John D.! We're going on an adventure!"

That's my uncle, Dr. David Harleyson: world-famous artist.

"You know, I've tried for years to get hold of that rascal Br'er Rabbit to add his portrait to my collection. Finally, today I have a letter back from Br'er Fox. He says he's happy to help me find Br'er Rabbit. Aunt Lill and I are taking the morning train to Sandy Creek, and we want you to come with us."

"Oh, Dad!" I said. "Please! School is out! I'll eat my vegetables, I'll brush my teeth, and I promise I'll write to you every day!"

Dad looked at Uncle and then he looked at me. "Okay, but mind your manners and *stay out of trouble!*"

"Hooray!" I shouted. "We're going on an adventure!"

J.D.H.

Tuesday, June 8

Dear Dad,

    It was fun being on the train. Every time the engineer blew the whistle, everyone would wave at us, and I waved back!

    Tonight we are staying with Br'er Fox and his family. I heard him telling Uncle, "I've known Br'er Rabbit for a long time. I'm mighty tired of being outsmarted by all his pranks and tricks. One of these days I'll get hold of him and teach him some manners."

    Br'er Fox is going to take us out looking for Br'er Rabbit in the morning.

    I hope we have breakfast first!

Love,

John D.

The Great Southern Railroad

Destination: Sandy Creek
Passenger: John D. Harleyson
Departure: June 8, 7:00 A.M.

D.H.

Wednesday, June 9

Dear Dad,

    This morning we were walking down the road when Br'er Fox spotted Br'er Rabbit. I guess Br'er Rabbit didn't want to be found, 'cause he took off running and ducked into a little ivy-covered tree-stump house. Br'er Fox started yelling, "Br'er Rabbit, open that door!"

    "Don't have time!" Br'er Rabbit said. "I'm too busy eating honey from my honey jar."

    "Mmm, honey," said Br'er Fox. "You know how much I love honey! I want some! Right now! Please let me in!"

    Br'er Rabbit said, all thoughtful-like, "Okay, but there's no room in here for both of us. When I step out, you step in. Then you can have ALL the honey that's in my honey jar."

CALAMINE LOTION
Pink to Stop the Itch of
Poison Ivy & Bug Bites
EASY TO USE, QUICK TO DRY.

As soon as Br'er Fox stepped in, Br'er Rabbit slammed the door shut. He dropped the latch and ran off laughing.

When Uncle unlocked the door, Br'er Fox stepped out holding Br'er Rabbit's honey jar. It was empty!

"Well, Br'er Fox," Uncle said, "no honey and no Br'er Rabbit! Let's go on back to your house. If you like, I'll paint YOUR portrait."

Tomorrow, Atticus Fox and his sister, Jane, and I are going fishing. I hope we pack a big lunch!

Love,
John D.

Friday, June 11

Dear Brother,

Early this morning we set off walking down the road to stay at Br'er Bear's. I don't mind telling you, it was hot!

At the front gate, Br'er Bear greeted us with a big smile. He said, "Come on in; my old friend Br'er Possum is here, and Ms. Bear and my daughter, Cleome, have lunch set out."

After lunch, Br'er Bear said, "I have a story for you, 'bout how Br'er Possum lost the hair on his tail."

"Yep," said Br'er Possum. "And Br'er Rabbit started the whole thing! He told me, 'If you're hungry, just go on over to Br'er Bear's and get you some persimmons. It's fine with Br'er Bear—he told me so!'"

Br'er Bear laughed. "Br'er Rabbit ran to tell ME you were in my persimmon trees STEALING my persimmons!"

TIONS TO BR'ER BEAR'S HOUSE

o out the front gate, turn left, and
the big red barn on your right.
Walk over the next hill. Then turn left at the next
left. Take the next road 'til you see
you see a row of five tall and you'll see a big oak.
house is on the la

Then Br'er Bear stopped laughing and said, "Seeing you in my tree, without even a howdy-do—it made me so mad! I shook that tree good and hard."

Br'er Possum said in a shaky voice, "You had me scared. I jumped out of that tree and ran!"

Br'er Bear shouted, "And I grabbed tight that bushy tail of yours!"

Br'er Possum looked at John D. and said, "Yep, and every hair on my tail was stripped clean off! That happened years and years ago, and my tail has been bare ever since! And all the tails of my children, grandchildren, and great-grandchildren look just like mine . . . no hair!"

I was laughing as I told him, "That's quite a tall tale, Br'er Possum. I'll be sure to put in your bare tail, if you let me paint your portrait!"

We're having fun. I'll write more later.

Love,

David

Sunday, June 13

Dear Dad,

This morning, Ms. Bear and Aunt Lill asked Cleome and me to pick some blackberries for a pie. We had just about picked our buckets full when we heard, "Good morning!" It was Br'er Rabbit! He was dangling from a tall, skinny tree. Cleome said, "Good morning, Br'er Rabbit. What are you doing up there?" He answered, "I'm scaring crows off this cornfield. It's fun! If you'll give me your bucket of blackberries, I'll let you get up here for a while."

I said, "Deal!"

Before Cleome could say anything, I bent down that tree, and pretty soon Br'er Rabbit was on the ground and I was dangling up in the air.

"'Bye, y'all!" said Br'er Rabbit, and he skipped off laughing with my bucket of blackberries. I was stuck, and I couldn't get down.

Cleome ran to get Br'er Bear. When he saw me, Br'er Bear was shaking his head. "John D., you've been fooled! You're in a trap Br'er Fox set to catch Br'er Rabbit, who's been helping himself to the corn in Br'er Fox's garden."

What an adventure, Dad!

Love,

John D.

P. S. After lunch and blackberry pie,
Uncle did a great painting of Br'er Bear.

Wednesday, June 16

Dear Brother,

It was pouring rain yesterday, and Br'er Turkey Buzzard was sitting out on Br'er Bear's fence. He wouldn't come in. He just sat there looking sad.

"Don't be worrying yourselves about me," he said. "Once this rain is done, I'm gonna build myself a big, fine house; then there will be no more sitting out in the rain for me."

When the rain was over, we saw him drying himself in the sun, spreading his wings this way and that, and laughing. "Rain's done! And it ain't gonna rain no more; no use in me building a house now."

Br'er Bear shook his head and said, "That ol' Buzzard—he ain't never gonna learn."

Love, David

P. S. Br'er Buzzard is coming by later today. I'm going to paint his portrait.

ael Harleys
Kenner Plac
adelphia, P

Thursday, June 17

Dear Dad,

This morning we had the best pancake breakfast! Aunt Lill and Uncle David were relaxing with their coffee when Br'er Wolf walked up.

In a big, deep voice he announced, "Suh, I am prepared to have my portrait painted!" This was a surprise, since Uncle hadn't asked him to come, but Uncle politely said, "Well, then, Br'er Wolf, let's get started."

I thought Uncle would never get finished. Br'er Wolf kept bouncing up to give his advice: "Make my nose smaller! My ears should be bigger! Make my whiskers longer!"

When Uncle sat back and said, "The painting is finished!" Br'er Wolf jumped up to look. "Mercy!" he said. "That's a handsome painting! It looks just like me!"

Love,

John D.

Friday, June 18

Dear Dad,

Ms. Bear made two big chocolate cakes today. We all ate and ate until every crumb was gone. Aunt Lill told me not to make a pig of myself, but I guess I did.

Uncle said he thought Br'er Rabbit must be a pretty smart fellow, since he could always figure a way out of trouble.

Br'er Bear said, "That's true, but there was one time Br'er Fox tricked him good.

"Br'er Fox decided to make a baby rabbit out of sticky black tar. He set it on a stump by the side of the road and took his self off to the bushes to wait and to watch. Pretty soon Br'er Rabbit came along strutting and whistling.

"Br'er Rabbit saw that tar baby sitting there and he says, 'Good morning! Mighty fine day we're having!' That tar baby didn't say nothing and Br'er Fox, he wasn't saying nothing.

"Then Br'er Rabbit says it louder, 'Good morning!' That tar baby wasn't talking, and Br'er Fox, he was grinning big.

"Br'er Rabbit said to that tar baby, 'Son, you'd better respect your elders and say good morning, or I'll have to teach you some manners!'

"Still that tar baby ain't saying nothing, and Br'er Fox was laughing up his sleeve.

"Br'er Rabbit, he gave that tar baby a clip with his right, and when that tar baby wouldn't let go, Br'er Rabbit gave him a clip with his left. Now he had both feet stuck to that tar baby. The stucker he got, the madder he got.

"Then Br'er Rabbit said, 'This is your last chance. I'm a-going to head butt you if you don't let go!' After Br'er Rabbit was stuck up to his ears, Br'er Fox, he came waltzing out of the bushes. He said, 'Well, well, well, what have we here? Looks like I'm going to have myself a barbecue tonight.'

"Br'er Rabbit, he started pleading with Br'er Fox. 'You can do anything you like—you can barbecue me, you can put me in a stew, you can bake me in a pie—but please, please, please don't throw me into the briar patch!'

"Br'er Fox thought awhile. 'Well, I don't have the wood to barbecue you, or the water to boil you, and it's too much trouble to fix a pie, so if the briar patch is the worst thing for you, then that's just where you're going to go.' He grabbed Br'er Rabbit by his ears and threw him as far as he could, deep into the stickery, prickery briar patch.

"It wasn't but a minute until Br'er Rabbit hopped out on the other side just a-laughing. 'Thank you, Br'er Fox! You forget I was born and raised in the briar patch. It's my most favorite place in all of Sandy Creek!'"

D.H.

Br'er Bear, his story told, sat back in his chair just as Br'er Rabbit came walking up with a big old grin and saying, "Folks are telling me you came to Sandy Creek just to find me."

"Hello, Br'er Rabbit!" said Uncle David. "Yes, it's true. For years now I've wanted to meet you and paint your portrait."

Br'er Rabbit laughed. "I'd be mighty proud to have you paint my picture. Come to my house in the morning. I'll be there."

Tonight I can hear Uncle; he's busy getting his paints and brushes ready for tomorrow and humming a little tune.

Love,

John D.

P. S. Ms. Bear gave me a big jar of honey; we'll have honey on our biscuits and pancakes when I get home. Yum!

Saturday, June 19

Dear Dad,

When we got to Br'er Rabbit's, he was waiting for us with Ms. Bear's bucket, full of fresh-picked blackberries. He whispered, "Good morning! I've just come back from picking these for you, John D. Now I'm standing here looking at my house and thinking everything seems mighty still and quiet—too quiet. I suspect somebody is in there waiting for me, hoping to get me barbecued.

"I'm going to find out who's in my house, without going in there. There are more ways to find out what's cooking than jumping straight into the stew pot!"

Br'er Rabbit climbed up on a tree stump and hollered, "HEYO, HOUSE!" Everything was quiet. Then he hollered again, "HEYO, HOUSE! WHY DON'T YOU ANSWER? YOU KNOW YOU'RE SUPPOSED TO HOLLER BACK, 'HEYO YOURSELF!'"

Then we could see somebody peeking out the window.
It was Br'er Wolf!

Br'er Rabbit hollered again, "HEYO, HOUSE! HEYO!"

Br'er Wolf tried to talk like he thought Br'er Rabbit's house would talk, and he hollered back, "HEYO YOURSELF!"

Br'er Rabbit gave us a big grin and hollered, "HEYO, HOUSE, WHY AIN'T YOU TALKING SWEET LIKE YOU ALWAYS DO?"

Then Br'er Wolf hollered back, just as sweet as he could, "HEYO YOURSELF, SUGAR PIE!"

We were all fit to burst from laughing and Br'er Rabbit called out, "Uh-huh, Br'er Wolf, that won't do. You could never talk as sweet as my house!"

That's when Br'er Wolf came slinking out and ran off down the road.

Br'er Rabbit shook his head and said, "I surely do hope one of these days Br'er Wolf and Br'er Fox will give up pestering me."

Ms. Rabbit and all the little Rabbits came out of the woods where they had been hiding. Br'er Rabbit gave them all a big hug.

Uncle said, "Br'er Rabbit, if you're ready, let's start the painting!"

It was late afternoon when the portrait was finished. We were all standing in the front room admiring it when Uncle said, "Finally, after all these years, I have what I wanted. With my brush and my paints, I'VE CAPTURED BR'ER RABBIT!"

D.H.

That's when Br'er Wolf and Br'er Fox jumped into the room! Br'er Wolf grabbed Br'er Rabbit and said, "Finally, I have what I'VE always wanted! I'VE CAPTURED BR'ER RABBIT, and this time we're going to have a barbecue!" Then Br'er Wolf and Br'er Fox were gone, with Br'er Rabbit held tight between them.

Uncle and I ran to help Br'er Rabbit and heard Br'er Rabbit laughing! Br'er Fox said, "We're about to barbecue you! Why are you laughing?"

Br'er Rabbit said, "I can't help it—I keep thinking about my laughing place, and I just have to laugh!"

Br'er Fox said, "Uh, I'd like to see your laughing place."

Still laughing, Br'er Rabbit said, "I thought you were going to barbecue me!"

Br'er Wolf said, "We can have a barbecue later. We want to see your laughing place NOW!"

"Okay," said Br'er Rabbit. "Follow me!"

Br'er Rabbit led the way through the woods. Finally he stopped and said, "See that hollow tree over there? Hit that tree good and hard and say, 'Laughing place, laughing place.'"

D.H.

Br'er Fox and Br'er Wolf marched up to the tree. With two big sticks it was BLAMITY BLAM and the tree shook, then it was BLAMITY BLAM again, and before they could say "laughing place" even one time, a zillion billion angry bees came boiling out of that tree.

Running, they shouted, "I thought you said this was a laughing place, Br'er Rabbit. WE'RE not laughing!"

Br'er Rabbit shouted back, "I said it's MY laughing place, and I AM!"

Br'er Wolf and Br'er Fox ran to jump in the creek with those angry bees buzzing right behind them! We could hear 'em yelling, "Ouch!" "Yipe!" "Ow-wee!" "Ow!" "Ow!" "Ow!"

Back at the house, we had to tell what happened five times!

Love,
John D.

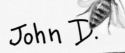

Monday, June 21

Dear Dad,

Last night there was a big party at Br'er Rabbit's. Uncle had all the portraits lined up on the front porch, and everyone was saying his portrait looked the best. Even Br'er Fox and Br'er Wolf were there, looking kind of shy with their bee stings all puffed up.

This morning, Uncle gave Br'er Rabbit and Ms. Rabbit a painting he had done of all the little Rabbits. Then the little Rabbits walked with us to the front gate, and we all waved good-bye.

Dad, we are at the Sandy Creek station waiting for the train. See you soon!

Love,

John D.

P. S. Remember the honey Ms. Bear gave me for our biscuits? Surprise, surprise! Somebody nibbled it 'til it was all gone—somebody with long ears!

Railroad

phia   Harleyson   1. 8:00 A.M.

oad

phia

avid Harleyson

21. 8:00 A.M.

The Great Southern Railroad

Destination: Philadelphia
Passenger: Lill Pigg Harleyson
Departure: June 21. 8:00 A.M.

D.H.

Ms. Jo Bear's BLACKBERRY PIE

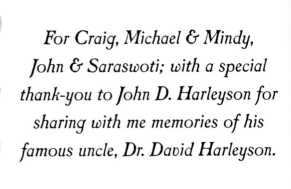

Preheat oven to 400°. Line a pie pan with pie crust. Mix 2⅔ T quick-cook tapioca into 1 C sugar. Blend this gently into 4 C of fresh-picked blackberries and let sit for 15 minutes before turning them into the pie shell. Dot the fruit with 2 T butter. Cover the pie with a top crust. Bake the pie in a 400°-oven for 10 minutes. Reduce the heat to 350° and bake about 40 to 45 minutes. Enjoy!!!

For Craig, Michael & Mindy, John & Saraswoti; with a special thank-you to John D. Harleyson for sharing with me memories of his famous uncle, Dr. David Harleyson.

AUTHOR'S NOTE

Many folktales have their origins in Africa and came to America with the people who were brought here unwillingly and enslaved. The hero in many of these stories was one of the weakest and least threatening of all animals, Brother Rabbit, or Br'er Rabbit. He was a mischief-maker who outsmarted the stronger animals with his wit and trickery, to the delight of a people who were struggling to retain their humanity, individuality, and joy in living.

Joel Chandler Harris wrote down many of the stories he learned from the slaves on the Turnwold Plantation in Georgia. Those tales were first published in 1880 as a collection titled *Uncle Remus, His Songs and Sayings*. Harris imbued them with stereotypes and nostalgia for plantation life. He is not the only writer to have published the retelling of these wonderful Br'er Rabbit stories, but he is the one that is most often identified with them.

Whatever his intentions, the publication of the stories has been a great gift to American literature. They are a written testament to the intelligence, inner strength, and deep spirituality of a people whose stories demonstrate their gifted storytelling ability and record their keen observation and understanding of both human and animal behavior. These folktales are part of the history of slavery in America and have been interwoven into the culture of America. It is my wish that through my retelling of some of these stories, the great contribution to literature made by the original storytellers will be remembered or discovered anew.

First published in the United States of America in 2007 by Walker Publishing Company, Inc. Distributed to the trade by Holtzbrinck Publishers

For information about permission to reproduce selections from this book, write to Permissions,
Walker & Company, 104 Fifth Avenue, New York, New York 10011

Library of Congress Cataloging-in-Publication Data
Cassels, Jean.
Br'er Rabbit captured! : a Dr. David Harleyson adventure / Jean Cassels.
p.   cm.
Summary: John D. and his Uncle David, the world-famous portrait artist, write letters reporting their efforts to
find elusive prankster Br'er Rabbit, aided by his favorite victim, Br'er Fox, and other familiar characters.
ISBN-13: 978-0-8027-9556-4 · ISBN-10: 0-8027-9556-0 (hardcover)
ISBN-13: 978-0-8027-9557-1 · ISBN-10: 0-8027-9557-9 (reinforced)
[1. Artists—Fiction. 2. Characters in literature—Fiction. 3. Portraits—Fiction.
4. Animals—Fiction. 5. Letters—Fiction.] I. Title.
PZ7.C268525Br 2007   [Fic]—dc22   2006101185

The illustrations for this book were done using gouache on 140-lb Arches hot press watercolor paper.
The text was set in Zemke Hand ITC, and the display type is Pluma Primeyra.

Visit Walker & Company's Web site at www.walkeryoungreaders.com

Printed in China
2 4 6 8 10 9 7 5 3 1 (hardcover)
2 4 6 8 10 9 7 5 3 1 (reinforced)

All papers used by Walker & Company are natural, recyclable products made from wood grown in well-managed forests.
The manufacturing processes conform to the environmental regulations of the country of origin.